THE GOLDEN COLLECTION

To everyone who helped fill my childhood with golden memories
Love you all

Contents

THE GOLDEN COLLECTION

SEHER FAISAL

Seher Faisal

Golden Poems

Introduction

The Golden Collection is a collection of poems I wrote in high school. I was struggling with the idea of my childhood coming to an end. You juggle a plethora of contradicting emotions when you are on the brink of adulthood, including fear, excitement, anxiety, and doubt. It can be quite terrifying when you're staring out at a thousand paths that lay before you. Amidst all the stress, you may find yourself clinging to your childhood, longing so badly to turn back time to an era of construction paper artwork, sidewalk chalk, shadow-puppets, and carefree play. I spent a lot of time reflecting on the most wonderful memories, encompassed in a golden haze similar to the daylight that would stream through my window every morning. And with all the reminiscing, soon my map became less blurry as I charted out my goals and dreams. I found my strength in my childhood and the many lessons I had learned. Golden memories filled in the cracks in my bones and my compass found its way. And I wanted to capture every beautiful lesson I learned in paper and ink.

So, I present to you, the *golden* era...

Childhood's Magic

Childhood glimmered in iridescent light

You were surrounded in a bubble for years

Unaware of the delicacy of your current state

A rouge breeze could have shattered the peace

The one that had glistened around you your whole life

Enhancing the world's vibrancy

And showing you the best side of everything

The sheen of the bubble warped frowns into smiles

It showed you colors for miles and miles

Wastelands grew tulips

And pirates crewed old ships

Mermaids flashed gold scales

In all your favorite fairytales

The ones you read in the meadow

While daylight illuminated the words

And made magic feel *real*

Once you ran through wildflowers

Wild and free

You knew nothing but laughter, dancing with glee

You left trails of dandelion puffs in your wake

Making wishes on the stars that glistened in the lake

You dove into stories, devouring every page

Forsaking responsibilities, and etiquette, and grace

That bubble wrapped you in the most precious gold

Trapping sunlight in with you, it streamed through your bones

It looped through your curls and shined through your eyes

As you howled at the moon and you reached for the sky

Until one day you reached too high

And your bubble popped and the sunshine flooded out

Leaving you alone in a frightening drought

The world barged in, and it was hard at first

To find your feet...it all felt like a curse

But once you realized you retained some magic

The gold in your bones helped you write your ballad

As you stole back the happiness childhood had held

And you danced through life, over waterfalls and hills

At every milestone you planted a flag

In shimmering opportunities you found yourself in this land.

Candles

Blow out the candles, close your eyes

Don't share your wish, keep it in your mind

I know you're stressing about running out of time

Darling I'll be here until the sunrise

Time slips through our hands

Like running water or golden sand

The candle's melting precious wax

Love, take a breath and count to ten

The candle burns, and before our eyes

Will disappear, leaving you and I

Wishing we didn't stress throughout our life

Wishing we took advantage of our time

So darling I'll be here until the sunrise

Time slips through our hands

Like running water or golden sand

The candle's melting precious wax

Love, take a breath and count to ten

When we're young we live in the moment

Now we divide time to find the right quotient

Some time for life and some time for you and I

Darling blow out the candles, we're all out of time.

Clouds, Dreams, and Impossible Things

I'll take a jar full of clouds and a pocket full of dreams as I travel to the stars where I'll achieve impossible things.

Dear Nanababa,

I remember sleepovers every weekend

And all the comforting hugs you'd lend

I remember driving for the first time with you

Your contagious, joyful laugh and sweet smiles too

And apple picking from your shoulders

I've got these memories packed away in a folder

They're kept securely in a very special place

Because they're the ones that bring a smile to my face

My childhood was made so much sweeter with you

You were always smiling and laughing and as I grew

I learned to do the same-I'd just keep smiling through the day

Because I always saw a gentle smile on your face

I wouldn't be who I am if it wasn't for you

I learned to be kind, work hard, and always tell the truth

And to cherish each and every second of life

If only you could see you through my eyes

You would see a role model to always look up to

Someone who has always been so precious to you

Because he's so strong yet so affectionate

Dauntless and generous, faithful and compassionate

Someone that you love *so so so* much

Because that's what I see-trust me it's true

Nanababa, happy birthday

And I love you more no matter what you say.

Daisy

Hey there sweet little Ayah

There's so much I want to tell you

You're growing up so fast

I blink, and another year has passed

I hope you know I'm proud of you

Of the way that you stay true to you

Your heart is much bigger than most

And it just continues to grow and grow

Like a daisy, bright and full of joy

You're brilliant and you're going far in life

And twenty years from now

I can see you at a podium, on a stage, or in outer space

Because you've got what it takes

Just what it takes to be great

You can play the game,

Raise the stakes,

Win the whole thing

Do you see what you can be?

You're my little daisy

Your laugh could cure my sadness

It's whimsical like magic

You're a shining star I hope you know it

So talented, yes go and own it

I've seen it myself you can do anything

Your determination is inspiring

My love for you is bright and golden

For my daisy bright and golden

You remind me of a garden

Whimsical and always growing

Beautiful and full of light

You could melt frozen hearts in a snap

Sprinkling golden magic just like sand

You're my little daisy

Forever my little daisy.

Daggers

They throw words like daggers

But at the end of the day

It's all background chatter

People are going to say what they want

They're going to spit poison when they talk

The only way to survive is knowing

Who's voice matters and who is lying

Acting like they know you more than you do

So you respond right through the tears you swallow

They were right when they said that words can leave you hollow

But they can also teach you that you're stronger than you know

So you need to get back up every time they bring you down

Because next time those words won't be able to knock you to the ground

They throw words like daggers

But at the end of the day

They don't really matter.

Fireflies

It's midnight when I look out my window

At the lights outside forming a halo

Fireflies twinkle out in the gardens

Beckoning me out into the darkness

They're hypnotizing with their golden lights

Blinking

Twinkling

Glittering

In the night

They are the stars in the lush green grass

And like headlights on a car they light up my path

They lead me out to a dream-like world

One without jobs and phones and wars

We dance alone in the lush green grass

And they make me a gown of golden lights

And I'm free for a moment from a world that demands

Too much of your time and too much of your mind

And the fireflies here seem to understand

That I want more in my life

Then work emails and dinner plans

I want gray skies and moonshine

Blue oceans and black sand

Seas to explore and mountains to climb

I want to dance in the rain

And not run from it

I want to live every day

And not stress about it

I want to thrive in the dark

And not fear it

I want to learn from mistakes

And not drown in them

I don't want to miss a single sunrise

Sunset, twilight, noon, or midnight

Stuck in a world that steals too much of my time

And too much of my mind

So I venture outside to the golden lights

Blinking

Twinkling

Glittering

In the night.

Gold

Like the stars in the night sky

Like wedding rings and sunshine

Like daylight through the tree line

Like gleaming sand on the shoreline

There's a golden gleaming bond

That's been shining for so long

Brighter than a shooting star

I found a friend worth melting for

Because I struck gold with you

Like the sunshine at sunrise

Like sunset in the evening time

Like a lion's radiant eyes

Like fire in the moonlight

Our friendship is a special golden

Like stars reflected in the ocean

Like fairy lights strung in the garden

Like sunrise every single morning

And I struck gold with you

Cheers to the late nights

Cheers to the good times

Out of a million souls

I was blessed with the best

I wandered into a gold mine

Nearly impossible to find

And there I found my best friend for life.

Golden Addition

By the time golden hour struck

I was in a wildflower field

The silver moon had glistened and shined

And the stars had listened to my celestial rhymes

I was engulfed in a peace so chaotic and loud

Epiphanies bloomed in this profound landscape

And I spent my time painting magical dreamscapes

I had stolen the word "whimsical" and it now orbits my soul

Along with the constellations of memories that I nourish and hold

I pulled myself out of the deepest holes

And swam upriver against currents and waves

And in the end I found in myself a gilded new strength

I inhale sunlight and exhale exuberance

I keep my childhood in the palm of my hands

And I am no longer frightened of uncharted land

My head and my heart dance in a balance

I had shattered them both into innumerable fragments

Now they are whole again, the scars bright and gold

And they follow maps of twinkling stars

All my love encompassed in crystal memoirs

Through folds of darkness I now prevail

With the moon in my eyes I can never truly fail

And golden hour's sunlight streaming through my bones

I'm thriving with the addition of this gold in my very soul.

Home

We bought a little house on Lexington Drive

Started calling it home once you arrived

Because when you came along the flowers bloomed

We ran and screamed to the sky, endlessly blue

And we tripped on the roots of a magnolia tree

And once we learned to fly we climbed the branches to the sky

At the top of the tree we thought nothing could reach us

Time couldn't touch us when our fingers scraped the sky

We wholeheartedly believed that for years and years

We woke up beneath dreamlike sunlight

And played in a room, blue as brilliant as the sea

An our imagination reached the very seams of reality

We glimmered in our bubbles

Iridescence shined in a rainbow world

But time rushes at you like a waterfall

And it chips at your youth with every sunrise

And by sunset I would find that I had discovered seven new colors

And eventually I would fall asleep under diamond shooting stars

It was an era of blissful naivety and childlike innocence

But as your world expands your home becomes too small

And you must find a new place to continue to grow

So once that chapter closed we found Wildflower Lane

The very first night the sun sank beneath the horizon

It was a glorious sight with clouds right out of a painting

And our new little home was painted in the dripping sunset

There was more space to run and everything was perfect

But new faces and schools were daunting and cold

We braved it for years until a storm unfolded

Doors and windows sealed shut and the world went silent

We stayed in our home and spent time together

A fire burned in the fireplace while we played games all night long

We grew closer in that time as the world weathered this storm

Against an illness that crept into so many homes

Ours stayed safe for the longest time

And soon we began to spend more time outside

And rediscovering our favorite fairy tales

Biking on new trails

Baking lopsided cakes

Playing loud board games

And rewatching childhood classics

We played like the old days and rediscovered magic

And those fortified bonds brought us out of the storm

They have never lost their glow even years down the road

We'll reminisce on the days laying on the trampoline

Laughing beneath the few stars that we could actually see

Ephemeral times hold infinite love and bliss

And the kind of happiness you know when you are just a little kid

I'll forever cherish those beautiful times

Because I know that chapters end all the time

Oh, but what I would give for a little more time

Once we were young-living in our own orbit

And now here we stand, once again silhouetted against the sunset

On the brink of the edge of an entire new chapter

Somewhere within the wild and whimsical we all grew up

And what a beautiful end to the most wonderful childhood it was.

Honey Skies

Honey skies in the summer

Golden sunlight through the shutters

Dragonflies out by the water

Butterflies through my window

Birds sing on my headboard

I don't understand a single word

But I dance anyway.

I'll Put You in My Pocket

"I'll put you in my pocket

And take you to work"

You bought a single silver locket

My name engraved in the heart

And a tiny box where I could lock it

To keep it safe from the world

You've always had the heart of a child

And the brightest of smiles

You've kept me safer than a promise

From a world that was heartless

You made sure we never saw it

So my childhood was golden and bright

Laughs and vacations and lovely sunlight

I love you

More than you know

I know it doesn't always show

I really hope that you know

That for you I'd change the world

You held our house on your back

Your smile never cracked

You taught me to swim

To fight and to always win

And you used to say

"I'll put you in my pocket

And take you to work"

You bought a single silver locket

My name engraved in the heart

And a tiny box where I could lock it

To keep it safe from the world

Daddy, I love you

More than you'll ever know.

Imaan

A butterfly with iridescent wings

Will go on to achieve impossible things

Through all the hardships she will prevail

Whimsical like a fairytale

And lovely like the sweetest dream

There is a fractured mosaic in her iridescent wings

Shards of love, resilience, and bravery

Give her the kind of beauty you can't help but admire

Ever changing like the seasons

She's stronger than she seems

Go, sweet butterfly

Take flight into the skies.

June Daffodils

Popsicle sticks and early mornings

Building castles with evenings exploring

Waterfalls and other planets

We had even ruled all of Atlantis

Fighting off the demons

And riding on the dragons

Imagination knew no limits

Back when we were just all children

January mornings and June daffodils

Sunday weddings and Friday night thrills

Yellow dresses and Tuesday evenings

Summer dances and winter feelings

Childhood memories and days full of dreaming

The warmth of your laugh

And your radiant smiles

I miss the times where we were living

Running, flying, and singing

Golden sunlight and sunny afternoons

Where I was living in the clouds with you

We were superheroes, princesses,

Elves, fairies and hobbitses

Our toys were our precious

Do you remember how we were restless?

Our imagination knew no limits

Back when we were children

Chocolate milk while the night was young

Pouring rain where we danced and sung

Laughing out loud throughout the night

Fireflies lighting up the sky

We had all the stars in our eyes

And our dreams were so bright

We felt so...alive

Oh, the warmth of your laugh

And your radiant smiles

I miss the times where we were living

Running, flying, and singing.

Just Breathe

Whispers carry in the breeze

Rustling in the autumn leaves

I listen, and they say to me

In gentle winds that caress my cheek

Oh my darling...just breathe.

Last Straw

You know now when I look back

At my trials, my failures, my bad days, my breakdowns

My first thought is that my last straw

Would have been about twenty straws ago

A decade ago

I could have given up

It seemed so rough

But I'm still here

I'm still standing here

Maybe I'm not as weak as I feared

Maybe I *do* have what it takes

Maybe I *can* win this whole game

Bask in the haze of happiness and success

Because if I think about it,

My last straw would have been twenty straws ago

But I'm still going

Yes, I'm still glowing

I'll find a way even if the tides grow higher

If there's one thing I know it's that I am a survivor.

Lost in Wonderland

I'm lost in wonderland

And I'm not ever going back

Because now I'm wading through the clouds

And watching waves crash up so high

I love the way they ripple blue above me in the endless navy sky

I'm dazzled by the diamond rain

And dancing like I've gone insane

In a gown made up of stars

Which show off all my faded scars

I'm feeling so alive

It's like I'm finally alright

I know I'm living in a fever dream

But it's better than reality

No stress, or work, or long sad days

It feels good to be away

Lost in my own imagination

Even if it's just a distraction.

Metamorphosis

On a chilly May morning a chrysalis shudders

A creature is emerging-there's something different about her

She stands on shaky legs with a newfound beauty and grace

Stretching the wings upon her back, still wrinkled in state

She takes her time as the sun warms her wings

Soon they'll be strong enough for her to do amazing things

She'll travel great distances, fly on for miles

A beauty to behold she's radiant like a smile

Eventually her wings extend and she flutters

A tiny step, not perfect, she takes a moment to recover

But she tries again and again getting stronger and stronger

She's almost ready now it won't be much longer

Her wings extend and she's dazzling in the light

Reflecting the sun on her golden wings as she takes flight

It took a brave step to leave her little branch

But now that she did it, now that she took that chance

She's seeing the world from new little eyes

As she flutters around endless honey skies

She knows her strength and she knows her power

She can feel it with every sip of sugary nectar

She is a majestic piece of living art

Like a fractured mosaic in the shape of a wing

And she's going to go on to achieve a million impossible things.

Only Fifteen

I may only be fifteen,

But there are still a thousand things this life has already taught me

Throughout all my experiences so far

I've realized that in order to live a happy life

Or fight through some incredibly tough times

You need to sit back and count your blessings

Or simply feel the beat of your heart

Just be grateful for every scar marking your arms and legs

They tell the story of your life

And for each illness which left your immune system fortified

For the chores that make your house a home

For the times you found that you were not alone

For every time you've fallen because it only fueled your determination

When from all that frustration you realized...it would be alright

Just let your taxes symbolize your employment

Let every mistake be a learning experience

Get up every time you meet the pavement

Let every tiny flutter take you higher

Let others' mistakes make you wiser

Let a far parking spot be a reminder

That your legs can carry you further than you think

Remember that…

When you hear that stupid alarm clock go off every morning

It marks another day that you are blessed with life

Let your heating bill remind you of your warm home

Remember that you have a family of your own

While millions of others live alone

And no matter what happens you can always turn to God

Just breathe, my love

It'll be alright

Now I may only be fifteen

And I'm still learning about this world and my deen

But I know for a fact that a good life requires you to look on the positive side

See the glass half full rather than half empty

After all, everything happens for a reason...believe me

Starlight and Diamonds

April's diamond showers

Brought the most beautiful flower

With a golden stem and pretty leaves

Crystal petals and shiny seeds

And she taught me to dream

About the most beautiful things

Touch the sky and spread my wings

Live with curiosity

But never reaching grandiosity

Because she never let them dim her light

She never let them kill her fight

She's glowing from the inside out

She's dancing to her own beat now

She painted skies of starlight

A dream in the dark night

Glittering so bright

April's diamond showers

Brought a woman who inspired

A daughter with a million dreams

To finally spread her wings

And become dream in the dark night

Glittering so bright

Spotlights reflect your beauty

In kaleidoscopes of rubies

So all the world can see it

You pull us up so high

So we twinkle right beside you

You're impossible to break

Like a brilliant little diamond

They can't look away

From your eyes glittering like starlight

You're stronger than diamonds

You're shining like starlight

Forever glittering so bright.

Summer Vacation

Sun kissed smiles

And iridescent bubbles

Dresses and messes

Of glitter and paint

Boxes we traveled in to outer space

Pink nail polish and bubblegum

Climbing trees in the summer sun

Cannonballs into pools

Fluffy clouds in a sky so blue

Bonfires and fireflies

Fireworks every July

Cartwheels on empty streets

Sidewalk chalk dust on our feet

Summer shined in golden days

In rain and shine we played and played

Sunset Journey

I'll travel when the sky's alight with colors

A dripping display of watercolors that decorate my wings

Fashioned with clouds and hope, they'll break barriers of sound

And lift me so high off the ground

That both my knees will scrape the clouds.

Sunshine Baby

Hey I've been loving lately

How you sleep so peacefully in the sun

Oh, you look so pretty

I love you my sunshine baby

And I've been thinking lately

About how you make me smile daily

And whenever my heart's aching

I look for you my sunshine baby

You're my sunshine baby

Your love is sunflowers and daisies

We look out the window when it's raining

Watch the flowers slowly blooming

You know you're like a pretty daisy

You're my joy my sunshine baby.

The Daisy, The Butterfly, and The Moon

Silver moonbeams cascade on the tree line

The gentle music of the magical night time

The butterfly glistens and glimmers in the moonlight

Resting on the leaves of the daisy's blooming green vines

There's a sense of serenity beneath the starlight

The moon glows silver, calm, and so bright

The butterfly flutters and lands so light

The daisy sways in the cool, sweet breeze of the night

A daisy brighter than a smile

A butterfly that'll travel miles

The moon so lovely, like a friend

A love that never ever ends

Wings so delicate but a will so strong

A flower so brilliant, dauntless, and young

A celestial object, shining so majestically

Together we exist, so wonderfully and chaotically.

The Struggle

Some nights are colder than others

Some days are just rain and thunder

Sometimes you can't fall asleep

Because the demons still creep

In the corners of your mind where only you can see them

Where they taunt you and tease you from the storms within

When no one else ever helps you

You're fighting this battle on your own too

Only you're never alone

Think of the truths you've been shown

And maybe someday you'll find a rainbow in your tears

Don't hesitate to cry when you're facing your fears

For tears aren't a symbol of weakness

But your humanity's realness.

Uncertainty

Growing up is clouded in gray shimmering mystique

And you venture through it with glaring uncertainty

As a child you dreamed of limitless opportunity

And now all your options begin to feel overwhelming

Will you regret every step years down the line?

Will you make something beautiful out of this life?

Will you dazzle among the elite in silver skyscrapers?

Or shimmer in the sunlight, where the ocean is your neighbor?

Do you chase the money or do you follow your dreams?

Your internal compass is spiraling and time just keeps passing

It's beautiful and yet terrifying, as your world comes tearing at the seams

And in the chaos you search for a place you'll find peace

But for now, your life is clouded in gray shimmering uncertainty.

Wild Child

In my defense the world is cold and I didn't bring a coat

I should have listened to my mother when she said to dress warm

I didn't expect the loathe the concrete jungle with all of my heart

I ache for the wild of the hills, the meadow, and the park

Shiny glass and sharp steel can never be evergreens tall enough to scrape the sky

I close my eyes and picture myself climbing up so high

I ran over roots and under branches as I chased the sun

But it always sunk behind a mountain that I could never cross

Canyons there still echo with my wildest screams

I cut both my hands and I scraped each of my knees

But I never stopped playing in the untamed weeds

I bathed in crystal streams

And I sang to the violets

And I shattered all the silence

Rules were a cage, and I wasn't prey

I lived for the thrill of freedom and play

So, when I can't fall asleep with concrete below me

And when I can't see the stars in a sky that looks smokey

And when I despise the city and long for daylight that's golden

And when I throw away my growing to-do lists

In my defense I am a child of the blue-sky wilderness.

When I Graduate

I haven't been outside in days

My hair is a mess, and my head aches

Staring at all these words on a page

That stopped making sense yesterday

I knew it wouldn't be easy

But I got overwhelmed so quickly

What if this is just not right for me?

Even though I want it so badly

I want to give this up so bad

Run far away never look back

But then I think about the day

Where I'll throw my cap and graduate

A degree that knows the sleepless nights

Every tear, failure, and sacrifice

That I made to get here

I'll throw up hands up as we cheer

So I open my textbook back up

Wipe my tears turn on my laptop

And I try and try and again

Until I make it to the very end

I just keep thinking about the day

I'll throw my cap and graduate

The cramps in my hand never stop

Because I keep writing, writing on

Knowing that I'll make me proud

When I wear that cap and gown

When I graduate.

Winter

I'll miss summer when it's gone

Its honey skies and golden sun

But I can't say that I want it to stay

Because for now the snow glitters all around

As frost crystals on the roofs of this icy little town

And the pale moon shines illuminating gray skies

As the sharp wind sings blowing through the icy rings

Summer may be a blessing, but winter is a miracle

A dead world turned into one that's so beautiful

I love the way snow flurries to the ground

Tiny crystals all fall from the sky without a sound

I love the way ice skates scrape against the frozen lakes

And the sharp wind stings against my cold pink cheeks

The cold fresh taste of falling snowflakes

And the frigid dry smell I think I'm under winter's spell

I can feel the cold chill my bones

And I can taste the snowflakes

I breathe in winter's scent

And hear the children cheer

As they're sledding down hills

Next to the snowmen that they built

Gray skies

Moonshine

Snowflakes

Ice skates

Winter is a dream with every snowflake

Frozen oceans

And snowed in again

Winter is a snow white heavenly place

Cozy coffee

And warm nights cuddling

Winter shimmers with every snowflake

And I'll miss summer when it's gone

It's honey skies and golden sun

But I can't wait for snowy winter days.

Wonderland

In Wonderland I wade through the clouds

To a sea of starlight glimmering all around

In the sky waves crash so violently

Crashing and moving so beautifully

Saltwater sprinkles down occasionally

From the whales as they breach so high above me

Where the moonlight reflects from somewhere below me

I look down where my feet are lost in the fluffy clouds

For the source of the moonlight shining all around

It feels cold but it feels pure

Like a silver shooting star

Then I spot it where it shines so majestically

Through the pink and purple clouds it calls to me

The moon looks brighter in Wonderland

A land where magic lives in the palm of my hand

The tiny golden sparks settle wherever

On my lashes and my shoulders

And they tangle in my hair

This place is a fever dream

So far away from reality

But I don't think I'll ever leave

Because here I feel like I can just *be*.

You

You stand tall like an oak tree

A home for so many

With branches to hold those that you love

And leaves to shield them all from the glaring sun

You bear all their weight

Even as your branches break

From the little ones who swing on the branches

Because they still think that they can grow wings

But you catch them every time

With a gentle laugh and a loving smile

And you tuck them in beneath your roots

And let them dream and dream while you

Watch over them throughout the night

Just as you have done for their whole life

You're someone they put their trust in

Because you stand strong like a mountain

So steady and calm

Blocking out the harsh winds until the break of dawn

You do all that you can to protect your whole family

Your sacrifices have never gone unnoticed

Your family loves you *so* much and they hope that you know it.

Your Smile

Iowa days on your shoulders spent out apple picking

Stray cats and long nights where we were all laughing

Days at the park and long evenings spent swinging

Elementary school parking lots where you took me driving

Your sweet gentle hugs whenever I was sad crying

Dominoes on the fireplace we'd send them all falling

Thank you for all of the sweet memories

Your smile is one of my favorite things

And to see it I'd do pretty much anything

So I write these poems for you

I love you more, despite what you say

My admiration for you is what I want to convey

You know you make me laugh every single day

And I love you more, despite what you say.

A Message From Me

The Golden Collection is a collection of poems I wrote around the time I was graduating from high school. It features childhood nostalgia, anxiety about the future, learning to live in the moment rather than stress about the future, and the golden haze I view my childhood through. The collection features many poems dedicated to the people I love, including *Dear Nanababa,, You,* and *Your Smile* which are dedicated to my grandparents, *Imaan, June Daffodils, Metamorphosis,* and *Daisy* which are dedicated to my sisters, *I'll Put You in My Pocket* which is dedicated to my father, and *Starlight and Diamonds* which is dedicated to my mother. Altogether, the collection showcases the many bittersweet emotions and the nostalgia that I was experiencing around the time of my graduation as I knew that my childhood was soon coming to an end. In this time of excitement, fear, hope, and uncertainty, it is important to always remember your strength. It's okay to fall back to your loved ones every once in a while, to feel the love of the people encompassed in a golden haze. The people who were with you from the very beginning. Draw your bravery, your determination, and your felicity from them and fall into dazzling sunsets on your journey to the stars. I believe in you, you're going to be just fine.

With all my love,

Seher

Acknowledgements

This entire collection of poetry is dedicated to my favorite people. If it weren't for their support, patience, and excitement I don't know if I would have been able to take this step and publish my first poem book. I love you all to the sun and beyond forever and ever. To Leena, a beautiful soul who knows me better than anyone else in the world. To Imaan, and her sparkling optimism and glimmering empathy. To Ayah, and her brilliant ebullience and wild determination. To my mom, and her whimsical joy and her infinite happiness. To my dad, and his infectious laughter and adorable smile. To my grandparents, and their unconditional love and their timeless wisdom. To my uncle and aunt, who always support and encourage me in everything I do. To Hiba, a huge inspiration and a huge help throughout the publishing process. And to my cats, Bucky and Kia, my sunshine babies who give the very best hugs. I'm beyond blessed to have each and every one of you in my life...I truly struck gold with you all.

Seher Faisal is a student at the University of Illinois Chicago studying Information and Decision Sciences. She has had a passion for writing ever since she could hold a pencil. Growing up with a vivid, overactive imagination gave her a love of storytelling through various formats. She hopes to build connections and make a wonderful impact on as many lives as possible through her work. In her free time, you can find her writing ardent poetry, catchy song lyrics, all genres of stories, or smothering her cats with kisses and love.